Jimmy Gownley's
AMELIA RULES!™

Amelia and the
Other Side of Yuletide

Atheneum Books for Young Readers
New York London Toronto Sydney

VISIT US AT
www.abdopublishing.com

Reinforced library bound edition published in 2011 by Spotlight, a division of the ABDO Group, 8000 West 78th Street, Edina, Minnesota 55439. Spotlight produces high-quality reinforced library bound editions for schools and libraries. Published by agreement with Atheneum Books for Young Readers, an imprint of Simon & Schuster Children's Publishing Division.

Antheneum Books for Young Readers
An imprint of Simon & Schuster Children's Publishing Division
1230 Avenue of the Americans, New York, NY 10020
Copyright © 2006, 2009 by Jimmy Gownley. Book design by Jimmy Gownley and Sonia Chaghatzbanian. All rights reserved, including the right of reproduction in whole or in part in any form. These comics were originally published individually by Renaissance Press.

Printed in the United States of America, Melrose Park, Illinois.
052010
092010
 This book contains at least 10% recycled materials.

Library of Congress Cataloging-in-Publication Data

Gownley, Jimmy.
  Amelia and the other side of yuletide / Jimmy Gownley. -- Reinforced library bound ed.
     p. cm. -- (Jimmy Gownley's Amelia rules! ; #4)
  Summary: At Christmas, Amelia and her friends in the G.A.S.P.--Gathering of Awesome Super Pals--are determined to discover the truth behind Santa Claus.
  ISBN 978-1-59961-790-9
  [1. Graphic novels. 2. Christmas--Fiction. 3. Behavior--Fiction. 4. Graphic novels.]
I. Title.
  PZ7.7.G69Al 2010
  741.5'973--dc22
                                                              2010006195

All Spotlight books have reinforced library bindings and
are manufactured in the United States of America.

With Love and Thanks
to Mom and Dad...

With appreciation for
the Vision and Faith of
Joe, John, Jerry, and Bill...

And with gratitude for
the Patience and Friendship
of Michael...

This book is dedicated with love...
for Karen.

Amelia and the Other Side of Yuletide

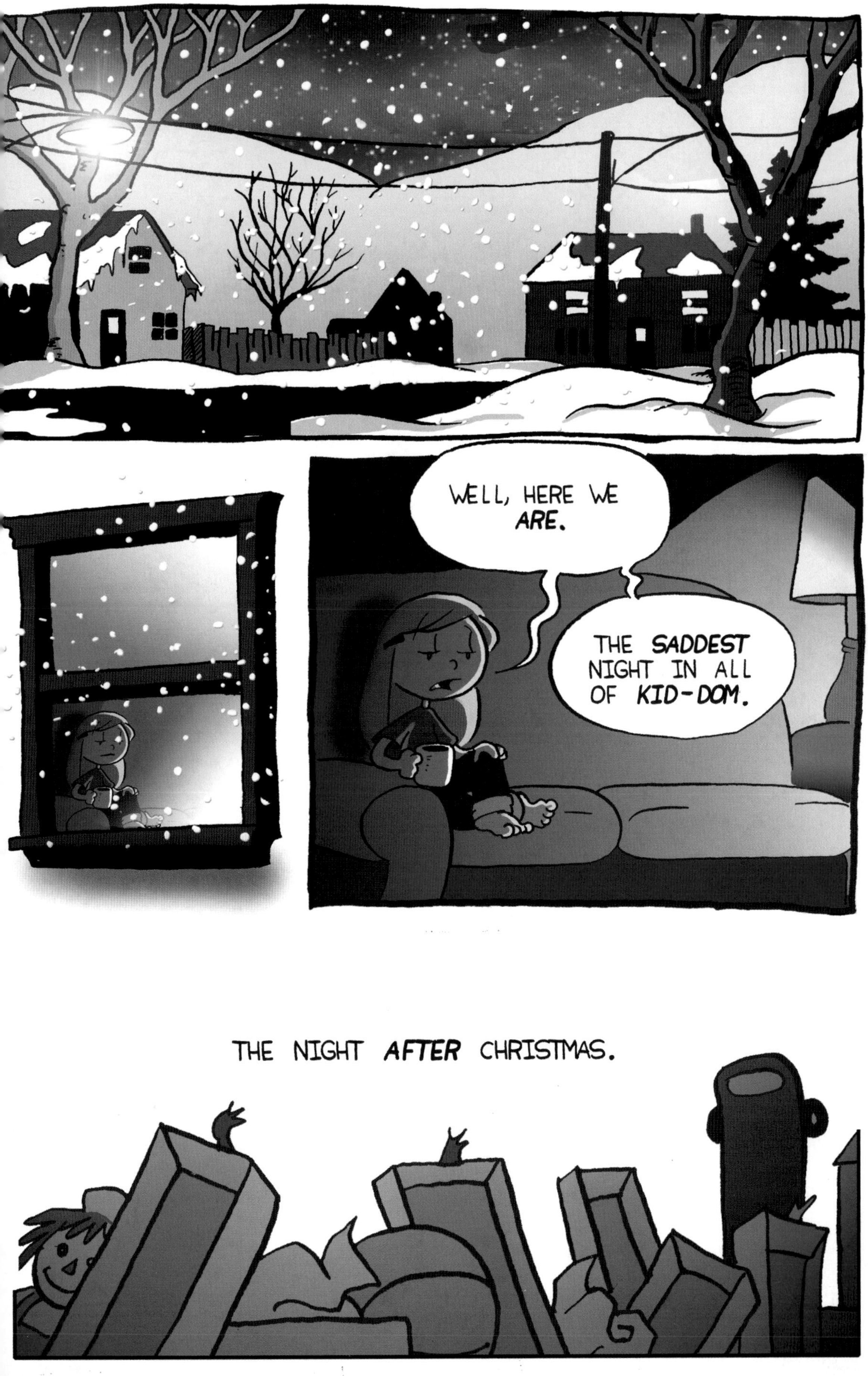
WELL, HERE WE ARE.
THE SADDEST NIGHT IN ALL OF KID-DOM.
THE NIGHT AFTER CHRISTMAS.

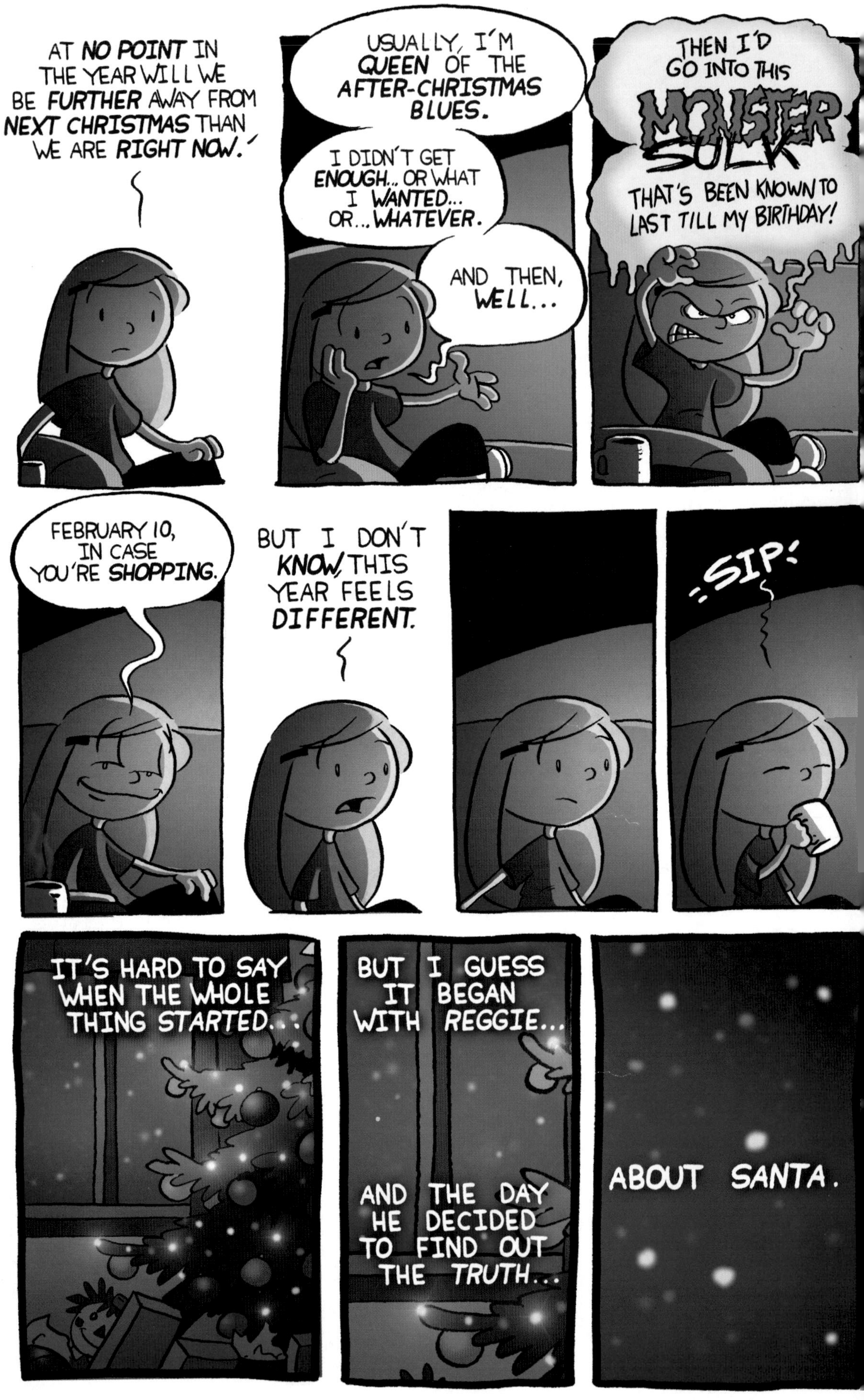
AT NO POINT IN THE YEAR WILL WE BE FURTHER AWAY FROM NEXT CHRISTMAS THAN WE ARE RIGHT NOW.
USUALLY, I'M QUEEN OF THE AFTER-CHRISTMAS BLUES.
I DIDN'T GET ENOUGH... OR WHAT I WANTED... OR... WHATEVER.
AND THEN, WELL...
THEN I'D GO INTO THIS MONSTER SULK
THAT'S BEEN KNOWN TO LAST TILL MY BIRTHDAY!
FEBRUARY 10, IN CASE YOU'RE SHOPPING.
BUT I DON'T KNOW, THIS YEAR FEELS DIFFERENT.
SIP
IT'S HARD TO SAY WHEN THE WHOLE THING STARTED...
BUT I GUESS IT BEGAN WITH REGGIE...
AND THE DAY HE DECIDED TO FIND OUT THE TRUTH...
ABOUT SANTA.

REGGIE COULDN'T HAVE PICKED A **WORSE** YEAR FOR THIS ADVENTURE.

IT LOOKED LIKE I WAS SET TO GRAB A **BIG HAUL**. I COULDN'T AFFORD TO END UP ON THE **NAUGHTY** LIST.

HMM.

OR WORSE YET...

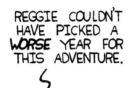

HO HO HO

Obnoxious, Nosy, Doofy

Amelia Louise McBride

OUT OF FEAR OF LOSING ALL MY **SANTA LOOT**, I DECIDED TO **REALLY** WORK MOM.

WH–WHY CAN'T WE BE A **FAMILY AGAIN**?

D–DON'T YOU GUYS **LOVE** ME?

IN MY FAVOR, I HAD THE IMPRESSIVE BUNCH OF BRIBES—ER, I MEAN, "GIFTS" FROM MY **DAD**.

BELIEVE ME, NO PARENT WANTS TO BE SHOWN UP BY THEIR **EX**.

SO, ARMED WITH A **TOYS 'R' US** CATALOG, I SAW MY **OPPORTUNITY**.

I DECIDED TO SELL IT **HARD**.

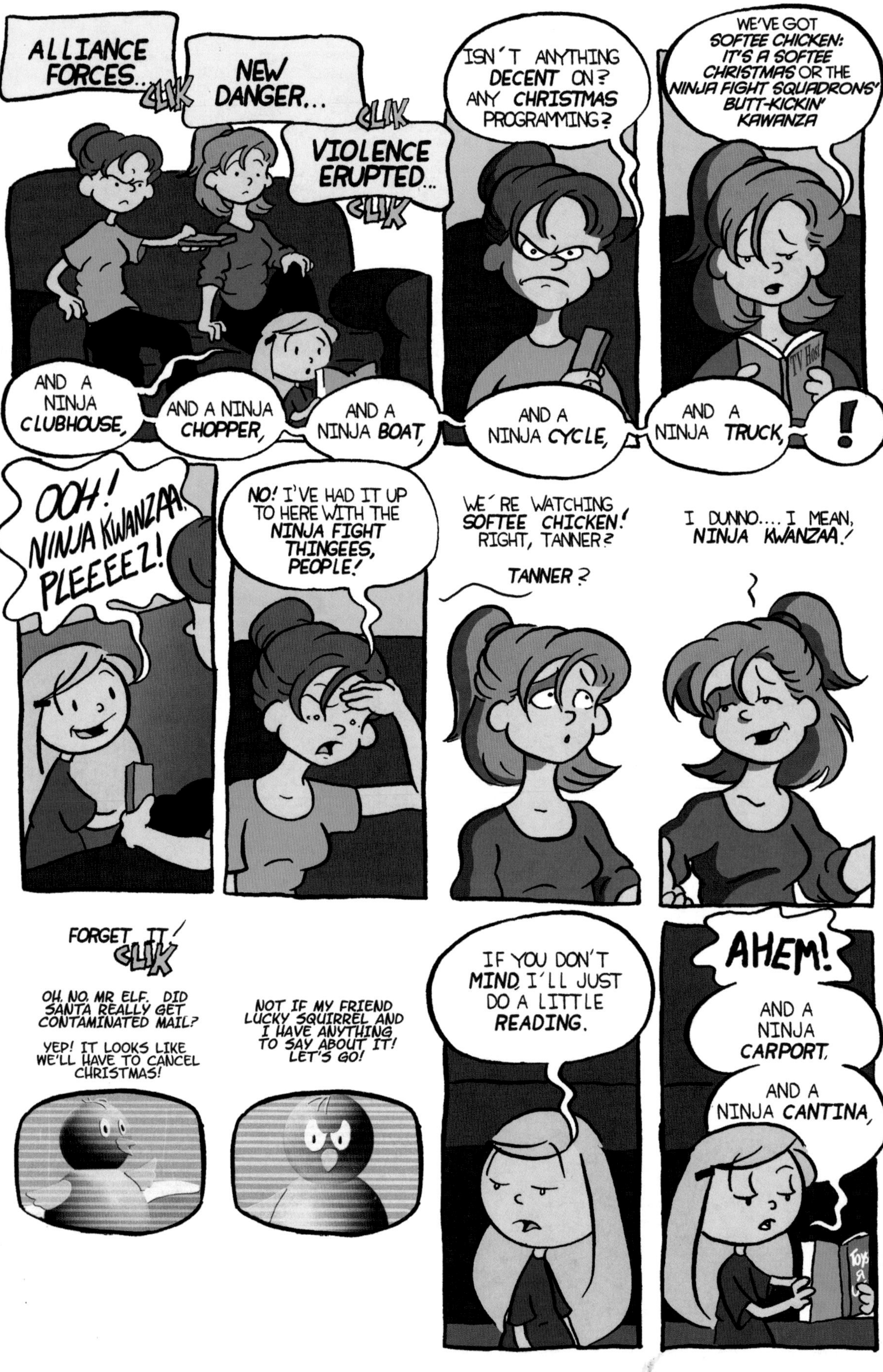
ALLIANCE FORCES...
CLIK
NEW DANGER...
CLIK
VIOLENCE ERUPTED...
CLIK
ISN'T ANYTHING DECENT ON? ANY CHRISTMAS PROGRAMMING?
WE'VE GOT SOFTEE CHICKEN: IT'S A SOFTEE CHRISTMAS OR THE NINJA FIGHT SQUADRONS' BUTT-KICKIN' KAWANZA
TV Host
AND A NINJA CLUBHOUSE,
AND A NINJA CHOPPER,
AND A NINJA BOAT,
AND A NINJA CYCLE,
AND A NINJA TRUCK,
!
OOH! NINJA KWANZAA! PLEEEEZ!
NO! I'VE HAD IT UP TO HERE WITH THE NINJA FIGHT THINGEES, PEOPLE!
WE'RE WATCHING SOFTEE CHICKEN! RIGHT, TANNER?
TANNER?
I DUNNO.... I MEAN, NINJA KWANZAA!
FORGET IT!
CLIK
OH, NO, MR ELF. DID SANTA REALLY GET CONTAMINATED MAIL?
YEP! IT LOOKS LIKE WE'LL HAVE TO CANCEL CHRISTMAS!
NOT IF MY FRIEND LUCKY SQUIRREL AND I HAVE ANYTHING TO SAY ABOUT IT! LET'S GO!
IF YOU DON'T MIND, I'LL JUST DO A LITTLE READING.
AHEM!
AND A NINJA CARPORT,
AND A NINJA CANTINA,

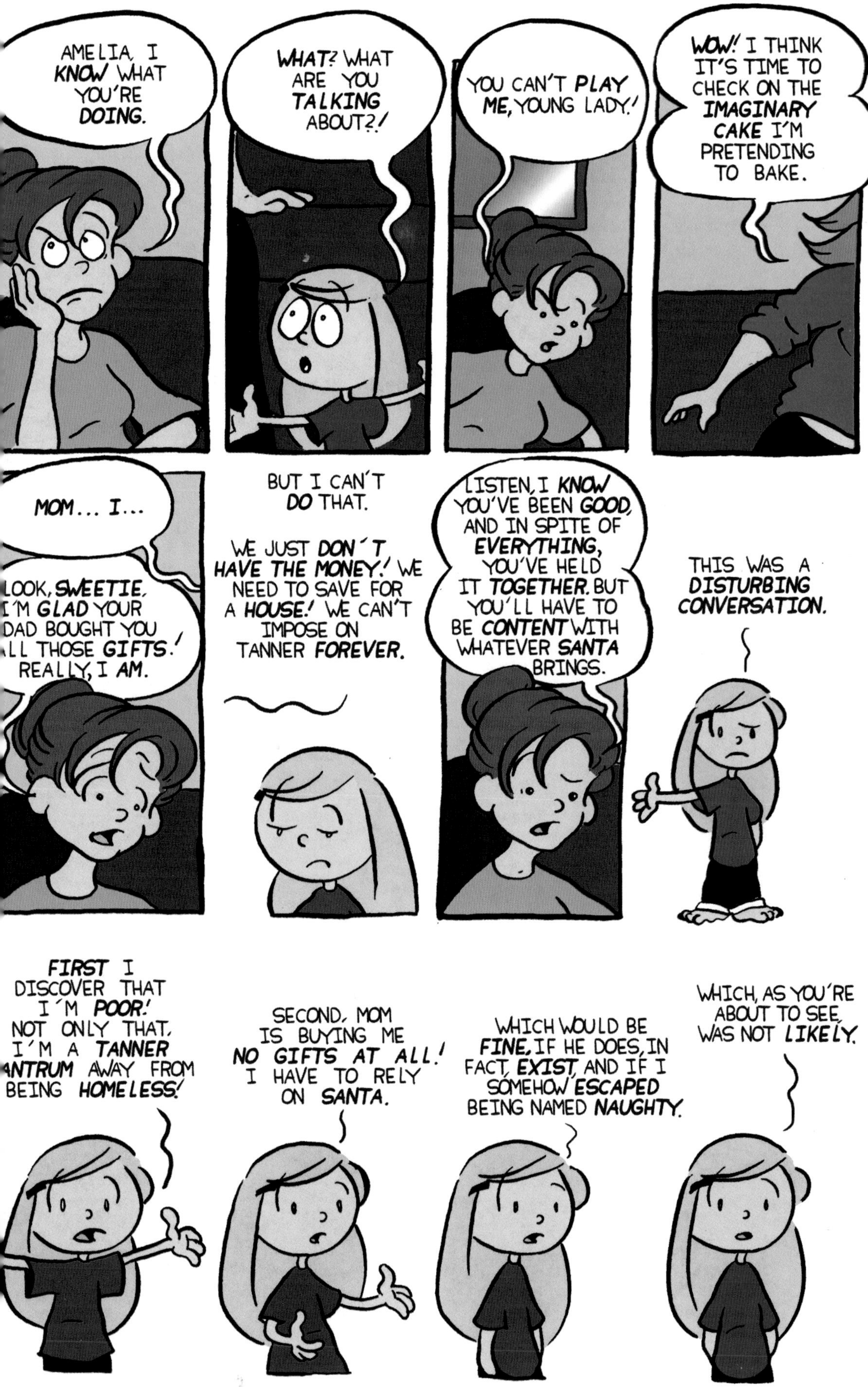

AMELIA, I KNOW WHAT YOU'RE DOING.
WHAT? WHAT ARE YOU TALKING ABOUT?!
YOU CAN'T PLAY ME, YOUNG LADY!
WOW! I THINK IT'S TIME TO CHECK ON THE IMAGINARY CAKE I'M PRETENDING TO BAKE.
MOM... I...
LOOK, SWEETIE, I'M GLAD YOUR DAD BOUGHT YOU ALL THOSE GIFTS! REALLY, I AM.
BUT I CAN'T DO THAT.
WE JUST DON'T HAVE THE MONEY! WE NEED TO SAVE FOR A HOUSE! WE CAN'T IMPOSE ON TANNER FOREVER.
LISTEN, I KNOW YOU'VE BEEN GOOD, AND IN SPITE OF EVERYTHING, YOU'VE HELD IT TOGETHER. BUT YOU'LL HAVE TO BE CONTENT WITH WHATEVER SANTA BRINGS.
THIS WAS A DISTURBING CONVERSATION.
FIRST I DISCOVER THAT I'M POOR! NOT ONLY THAT, I'M A TANNER TANTRUM AWAY FROM BEING HOMELESS!
SECOND, MOM IS BUYING ME NO GIFTS AT ALL! I HAVE TO RELY ON SANTA.
WHICH WOULD BE FINE, IF HE DOES, IN FACT, EXIST, AND IF I SOMEHOW ESCAPED BEING NAMED NAUGHTY.
WHICH, AS YOU'RE ABOUT TO SEE, WAS NOT LIKELY.

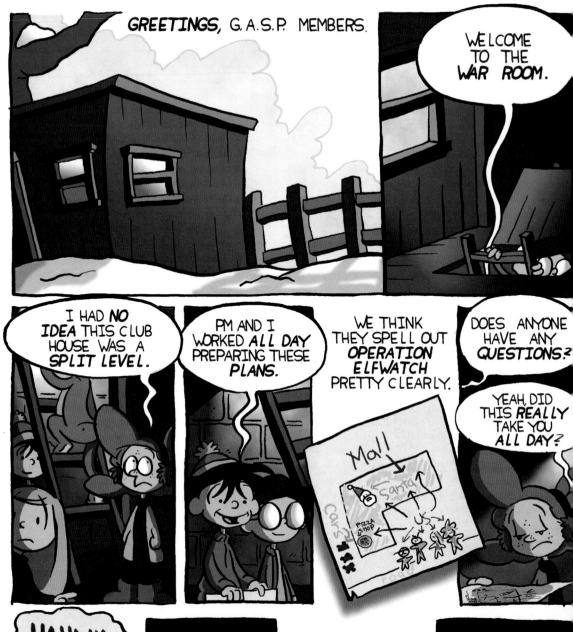

GREETINGS, G.A.S.P. MEMBERS.

WELCOME TO THE **WAR ROOM**.

I HAD **NO IDEA** THIS CLUB HOUSE WAS A **SPLIT LEVEL**.

PM AND I WORKED **ALL DAY** PREPARING THESE **PLANS**.

WE THINK THEY SPELL OUT **OPERATION ELFWATCH** PRETTY CLEARLY.

DOES ANYONE HAVE ANY **QUESTIONS?**

YEAH, DID THIS **REALLY** TAKE YOU **ALL DAY?**

HA HA HA

ARE THERE ANY **OTHER** QUESTIONS?

THAT AREN'T SARCASTIC!

LATER THAT AFTERNOON WE STOPPED BY **PAJAMAMAN'S HOUSE**. I HAD NEVER BEEN THERE BEFORE, AND IT WASN'T WHAT I **EXPECTED**.

THE PLACE WAS **TINY** AND KIND OF A **MESS**. IT WAS PRETTY **OBVIOUS** HIS FOLKS DIDN'T HAVE MUCH **MONEY**. I HAD BEEN FEELING SORTA SORRY FOR MYSELF AFTER WHAT MY MOM SAID, BUT SUDDENLY I WAS FEELING PRETTY **LUCKY**.

WHILE PM WAS OUT OF THE ROOM, I NOTICED THIS **CLIPPING** FROM A CATALOG TAPED TO THE FRIDGE. IT CAUGHT MY EYE CUZ IT WAS FOR THE **RED CAPTAIN NINJA** THAT WAS AT THE TOP OF **MY** WANT LIST. I REALLY THOUGHT DAD WOULD **COME THROUGH** WITH IT, BUT I GUESS THEY'RE PRETTY HARD TO FIND.

Latchicus Keykidius (the Common Latchky Kid) The Latchkys were a group of children descended from Polish nobility who lived in Warsaw durring the time of the Cold War. To protect themselves from the freezing temperatures brought on by this war, they wore big hats (fig. 1). Disgusted by their treatment at the hands of Communism, and appalled by the state of modern polka music, the Latchkys fled Warsaw in the middle of the night (fig. 2). Not being able to afford passage on a ship, the Latchkys were forced to swim the icy Atlantic, buffered from the elements only by their brains, their raw courage, and their big hats (fig. 3).

Upon finally reaching the shores of America, the Latchkys quickly forgot their past hardships, and, throwing off their waterlogged clothing, danced Butt Nekkid (except of course for the hats) in the streets (fig. 4). Their descendents (including Pajamaman) live in the US to this day, where they remain free to express their love of liberty, polka, and big hats.

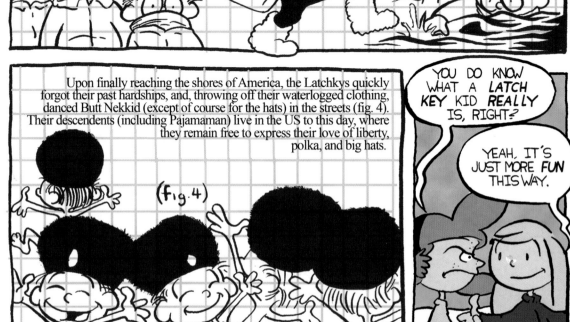

THINGS WENT ON AS USUAL, AND CHRISTMAS KEPT GETTING *CLOSER.*

BUT NO MATTER *WHAT,* I COULDN'T STOP THINKING ABOUT *PAJAMAMAN'S HOUSE* AND THAT STUPID CLIPPING.

I ASKED *REGGIE* ABOUT IT, AND HE SAID PM WAS PROBABLY *HINTING* THAT HE WANTED IT FOR *CHRISTMAS...*

BUT THERE WAS NO CHANCE HE WOULD GET IT.

IT WAS *WEIRD.*

I WAS JUST USED TO THESE GUYS BEING MY FRIENDS. I NEVER THOUGHT ABOUT WHO WAS RICH OR POOR.

AND EVEN THOUGH I FELT *BAD* FOR PM, I STILL *REALLY WANTED* A MOUNTAIN OF PRESENTS FOR *ME.* WHICH PROBABLY PUT ME AT THE TOP OF A *NEW LIST....*

ADD TO THIS THE NAGGING QUESTION OF WHY SANTA WOULD IGNORE SOMEONE LIKE PAJAMAMAN, AND THERE WAS ONLY ONE THING I COULD DO....

WHEN I WAS A KID, I REALLY LIKED THIS SONG, "STILL ROCK 'N' ROLL TO ME."

IT'S BY BILLY JOEL, AND ONE OF THE REASONS I LIKED IT, THE BIG REASON, REALLY, WAS ONE LINE:

"YOU SHOULDN'T TRY TO BE A STRAIGHT-A STUDENT IF YOU ALREADY THINK TOO MUCH."

HEH, HEH THAT'S PRETTY GOOD.

I THOUGHT SO! IT WAS, LIKE, MY MOTTO FOR YEARS!

♪ WHATSAMATUH WITDA CLOTHES AHM WEARIN'? ♪

BUT THE THING IS, ONE DAY I READ THE LYRICS AND THEY WERE COMPLETELY DIFFERENT!

"SHOULD I TRY TO BE A STRAIGHT-A STUDENT? IF YOU ARE, THEN YOU THINK TOO MUCH."

I WAS DEVASTATED!

I-I CAN'T GO ON.

BUT EVEN KNOWING THE NEW LYRICS, IT NEVER REPLACED THE ONE I'D MADE UP!

DO YOU KNOW WHAT I'M SAYING?

UM... YEAH. SANTA IS LIKE BILLY JOEL...ARE AND THE LYRICS ARE RUDOLPH, AND...

ACTUALLY, NO.

ALL I CAN *TELL* YOU IS WHAT *I* THINK.

AND THE *TRUTH IS,* I BELIEVE IN SANTA *NOW,* PROBABLY *MORE* THAN WHEN I WAS *LITTLE*

THERE IS REAL *MAGIC* AT CHRISTMAS, YA *KNOW?* I MEAN, IT'S COMPLETELY *CORNY,* AND I'D PROBABLY BE STRIPPED OF MY REPLACEMENTS *FAN CLUB MEMBERSHIP* FOR SAYING SO, BUT IT'S *TRUE.* AND ANY TIME YOU *FIND* MAGIC IN THIS WORLD, YOU HAVE TO *FIGHT HARD* TO KEEP IT.

I THINK WHAT YOU'RE *REALLY* ASKING, THOUGH, IS WHY ISN'T LIFE *FAIR?* AND I'M *SORRY,* SWEETIE, BUT I DON'T HAVE AN *ANSWER.* BUT LISTEN, YOU SHOULDN'T HAVE SUCH A *HEAVY HEART* ON CHRISTMAS EVE. SO *CLOSE YOUR EYES,* AND BE *CERTAIN* THAT SANTA IS ON HIS WAY.

AND WHEN YOU *SLEEP,* DREAM OF ALL THE *GIFTS* YOU *WILL* RECEIVE.

AND THE ONES YOU *ALREADY HAVE.*

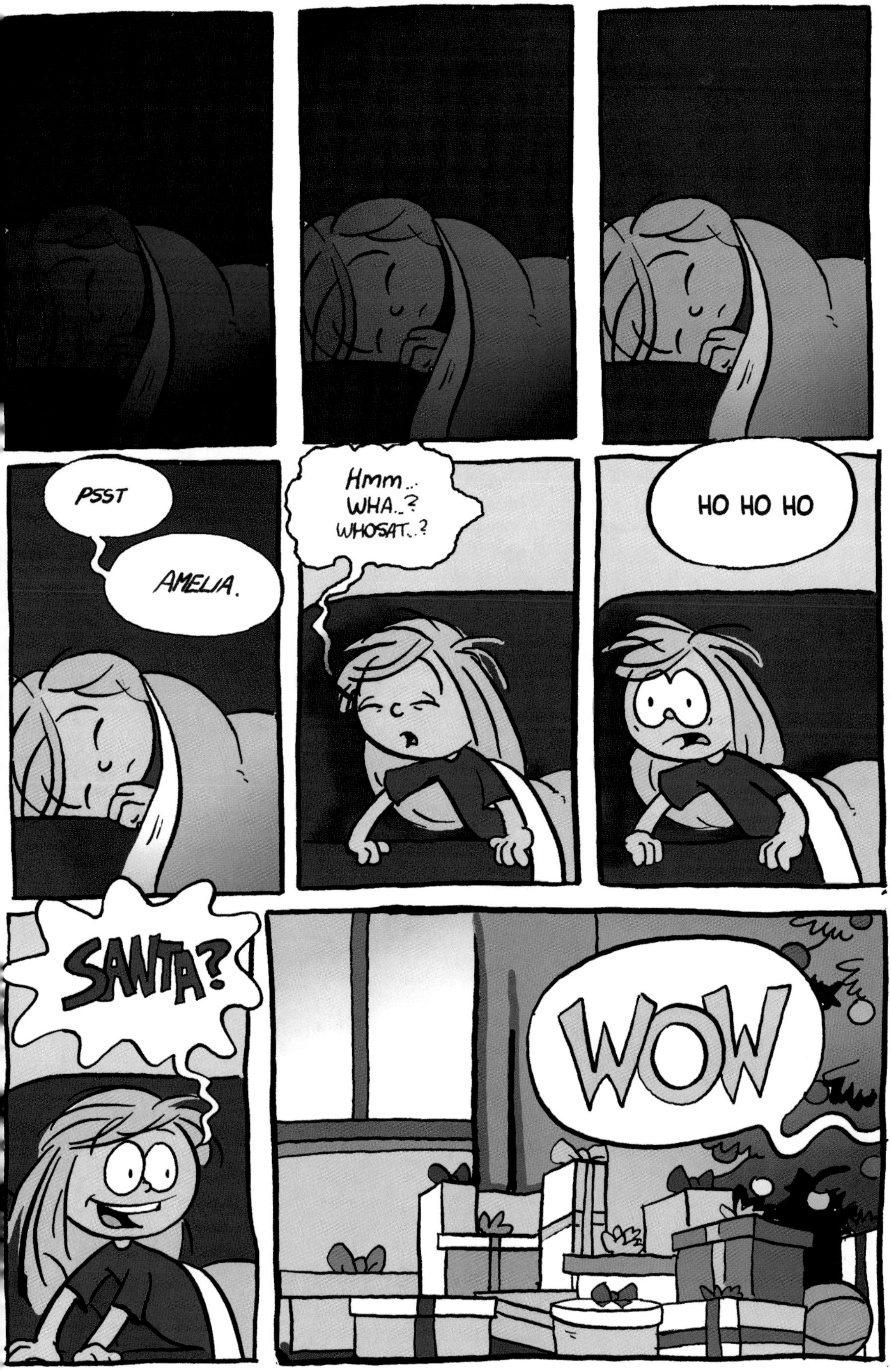
PSST
AMELIA.
Hmm..
WHA..?
WHOSAT..?
HO HO HO
SANTA?
WOW

I RULE!

I KNEW THE FAT GUY WOULDN'T LET ME DOWN! NOW LET'S SEE... HOW ABOUT WE START WITH...

THIS ONE!

RIP TEAR SHRED TEAR RIP

A HAT? LET'S HOPE THIS IS A LITTLE ELFIN HUMOR.

AH, THIS LITTLE BEAUTY IS A KEEPER. I CAN FEEL IT!

RIP TEAR SHRED TEAR RIP

I CAN'T *BELIEVE* YOU GOT *RED* CAPTAIN NINJA!

HEY, GUYS. WHAT'S UP?

AMELIA, COME ON IN! YOU WON'T BELIEVE WHAT HAPPENED!

THERE IS A SANTA! PM PROVED IT!

HE *SAW* *HIM* LEAVING HIS *HOUSE!*

HE SAID HE WAS KINDA *SHORT,* BUT IT WAS *DEFINITELY HIM!*

HE EVEN *DROPPED* HIS *HAT!*

"THERE IS A SANTA CLAUS."

HEARING THAT MADE ME *HAPPIER* THAN I'D BEEN IN A *LONG* TIME.

CUZ *LAST* CHRISTMAS, I LIVED WITH MY MOM *AND* DAD ON WEST 86TH STREET IN *MANHATTAN*.

NOW, I LIVE WITH MY MOM AND *HER SISTER* IN, LIKE, *NOWHERE*, PENNSYLVANIA.

AND THAT'S *FINE*. REALLY IT *IS*.

IT'S JUST THAT SOMETIMES I *MISS* THE WAY THINGS *USED* TO BE.

AND I *WISH* THAT I COULD GO *BACK*.

BUT, *REALLY*, I KNOW THAT EVEN IF I *COULD*...

BUT *ENOUGH* OF THAT. *THIS* TIME WE'RE HAVING A *HAPPY* ENDING!

IT WOULDN'T BE THE SAME.